SHOOTING
STAR

'Shooting Star'
An original concept by Katie Dale
© Katie Dale

Illustrated by John Lund (Beehive Illustration)

Published by MAVERICK ARTS PUBLISHING LTD
Studio 3A, City Business Centre, 6 Brighton Road,
Horsham, West Sussex, RH13 5BB
© Maverick Arts Publishing Limited November 2018
+44 (0)1403 256941

A CIP catalogue record for this book is available at the British Library.

ISBN 978-1-84886-391-0

www.maverickbooks.co.uk

This book is rated as: Gold Band (Guided Reading)

SHOOTING
STAR

By **Katie Dale**
Illustrated by **John Lund**

Chapter 1

Stella Smith was just like every other girl her age except for three things:

1) Stella couldn't walk. But that didn't bother her. She loved whizzing around on her wheelchair.

2) Stella was adopted. But that didn't bother her either. She loved her adoptive parents Mr and Mrs Smith, and they loved her.

3) Stella could fly!
She loved soaring up to
the ceiling and doing loop-the-
loops around the lampshade.

The only problem was, Stella had to
keep her flying secret.

"If anyone finds out, they might take you
away," said Mr Smith.

"Or experiment on you," added Mrs Smith.

"Or put you in a zoo," said Mr Smith.

Stella gulped. She was very careful. Whenever she went outside she used her wheelchair. She never flew in public, and no one suspected a thing. But Stella wished she could fly in the big blue sky.

One day, Stella's neighbour's cat got stuck up a tree. The tree was so tall, even the fire brigade couldn't get poor Tibbles down.

Stella bit her lip. She knew she could easily fly up and rescue Tibbles, but she couldn't let anyone see her powers! Then she had an idea.

Stella got out a sewing machine and her old swimsuits and leotards... and she made a disguise! She flew up and rescued Tibbles, and no one knew who she really was. Except Mr and Mrs Smith.

"You're a superheroine!" cried Mr Smith.

"We always knew you were special," said Mrs Smith with a smile. "Ever since you fell from the night sky and crash-landed in our garden when you were baby!"

"That's it!" Stella cried. "I'll call myself 'Shooting Star'!"

Chapter 2

After saving Tibbles, Stella got a real taste for being a superheroine. It felt so good to fly free at last! And it felt even better to help people in need.

She rescued cats from trees, helped people in trouble at sea, and even caught robbers!

"Thank you, Shooting Star!" everyone called.

One night, Stella was so busy saving people that she didn't get home until morning. She just had time to get changed and grab some breakfast before heading to school. But she was so tired that she fell asleep in her last lesson!

"Stella Smith, I hope we aren't boring you!" snapped her teacher, Ms Grey.

"Um, no!" Stella said quickly, waking up.

"Then can you tell me what this is?" Ms Grey held up a metal box.

"It's a…" Stella tried to guess. "A lunch-box?"

The rest of the class laughed. Ms Grey did not.

"It is a time capsule," Ms Grey said sternly. "It was buried on the school field ten years ago and we have just dug it up. Now come over, everyone, and have a look at what's inside."

Everyone gathered around the time capsule. Inside there were...

Some old coins and notes, a class photograph, a stamped envelope with a class letter about everything that had happened that year and a newspaper with the headline 'WHERE IS BURGLAR BIGGINS' BANK BOOTY?'

Stella picked up the paper to read the whole news story.

The newspaper said that a man called Bob Biggins had robbed a bank. But the money he had stolen had gone missing. It was a mystery.

"I wonder if they ever found the money?" Stella thought, aloud.

"Silence!" Ms Grey snapped, just as the bell rang.

Home-time! At last Stella could go home for a nap!

"Not so fast, Stella," Ms Grey said. "I'm afraid you will be staying late after your bad behaviour."

Stella groaned. It wasn't her fault she'd fallen asleep - she'd been up all night helping people! But she couldn't exactly explain that to Ms Grey.

Chapter 3

As the rest of the class left, Ms Grey gave Stella a piece of paper.

"Your task is to write a description of all the contents of this box," she said.

Stella sighed. Ms Grey clicked on the radio and started her marking.

Stella picked up the envelope, read the class

letter, then frowned. The letter was written to be put in the time capsule. It had never been posted – so why did it need an envelope and a pretty stamp? Very odd.

Stella moved on to the photo. It was strange to think that ten years ago these kids were sitting in this classroom. She peered at the names beneath the picture.

Jenny Mulroney, Fred Harris, Billy Biggins... Stella frowned.

No way... could Billy be a relative of Bob Biggins, the bank robber?

Suddenly the radio news came on.

"Police are still searching for escaped burglar Bad Bob Biggins," the announcer said.

Stella looked up sharply.

"Biggins escaped from jail this morning," the announcer continued. "Police have warned the public not to approach him, as he is a very dangerous criminal."

Stella grabbed her bag with her costume inside and headed for the door. This was a job for Shooting Star!

"Where do you think you're going?" Ms Grey said crossly.

"Um, to the loo," Stella said quickly.

"With your bag?" Ms Grey said suspiciously. "I'm not that silly. Finish your report."

Stella bit her lip. She had to find a way to transform into Shooting Star, and catch Bad Bob Biggins before somebody got hurt!

Just then, the door burst open. Stella gasped. Even Ms Grey's mouth dropped open. It was Bad Bob Biggins!

Chapter 4

"Get out!" Ms Grey shouted. "This is my classroom!"

"And this is my robbery!" Bob yelled, snatching the envelope from the time capsule.

"What do you want with an old envelope?" Stella asked, confused.

Bob laughed. "It's not the old envelope I want, it's the old stamp! It's very, VERY old! So old it's priceless!"

"That's how you hid your money!" Stella gasped. "You used the bank money to buy a priceless stamp and got your son Billy to bury it in the school field!"

"Clever girl," Bob said, grinning. "When I saw on the school website that you were digging the time capsule up today I had to come and get my precious stamp."

"You'll never get away with this!" Ms Grey cried. "Shooting Star will stop you!"

"Oh, be quiet," Bob said, tying her up.

Stella thought hard. If she flew across the room, she could quickly grab the stamp and rescue Ms Grey. But she couldn't fly without her costume on, because her secret identity wouldn't be secret anymore! What should she do?

Bob turned to Stella with another piece of
rope, then stopped and laughed.

"I don't need to tie you up," he grinned.
"You're just a kid in a wheelchair!"

Stella scowled as he ran from the room, then
raced after him. She just needed somewhere
private to transform into Shooting Star...

But the corridor was full of kids leaving after
school clubs! Stella hurried into the loos, but
there were more kids in there! Stella
panicked.

There was nowhere to transform!

Chapter 5

Powers or no powers, Stella couldn't let Bob get away. She hurried outside and spotted him running down the busy street. Stella pushed hard, but she couldn't keep up in her wheelchair...

Then Bob ran down a hill. Stella smiled.

Bob sprinted as fast as he could, but Stella's wheelchair was faster! She zoomed down

the hill, dodging rubbish bins and lampposts. Her wheels were a blur as she got faster and faster, until finally...

She swerved and ran over Bob's foot!

"YEEOWWWW!" Bob yelped. He hopped around, clutching his foot, and dropped the envelope!

Stella grabbed it, just as a police car
screeched to a stop beside them.

Bob tried to run, but his foot hurt too much
and a policeman soon caught up with him.

"Ouch!" Bob yelled. "I should have tied you
up too, little girl!"

"Never underestimate a kid in a wheelchair," Stella said, grinning.

"This is Bad Bob's hidden money!" Stella cried, handing the police the priceless stamp.

"Well done!" the police officer said as they handcuffed Bob. "Sorry we took so long. We're used to Shooting Star catching bad guys for us! I wonder why she didn't come this time?"

Stella smiled a secret smile. "I guess sometimes you don't need superpowers to save the day!"

The End

Book Bands for Guided Reading

The Institute of Education book banding system is a scale of colours that reflects the various levels of reading difficulty. The bands are assigned by taking into account the content, the language style, the layout and phonics. Word, phrase and sentence level work is also taken into consideration.

Maverick Early Readers are a bright, attractive range of books covering the pink to white bands. All of these books have been book banded for guided reading to the industry standard and edited by a leading educational consultant.

Pink
Red
Yellow
Blue
Green
Orange
Turquoise
Purple
Gold
White

To view the whole Maverick Readers scheme, visit our website at

www.maverickearlyreaders.com

Or scan the QR code above to view our scheme instantly!